Johnny Chuck did n't stop to think that
Reddy Fox was twice as big as he.

BURGESS TRADE QUADDIES MARK

OLD
MOTHER WEST WIND

BY
THORNTON W. BURGESS

Illustrated by George Kerr

GROSSET & DUNLAP
Publishers   New York
By arrangement with Little, Brown and Company

PRINTED IN THE UNITED STATES OF AMERICA

CONTENTS

LIST OF ILLUSTRATIONS

I

MRS. REDWING'S SPECKLED EGG

OLD MOTHER WEST WIND

I

MRS. REDWING'S SPECKLED EGG

OLD MOTHER WEST WIND came down from the Purple Hills in the golden light of the early morning. Over her shoulders was slung a bag — a great big bag — and in the bag were all of Old Mother West Wind's children, the Merry Little Breezes.

Old Mother West Wind came down from the Purple Hills to the Green Meadows and as she walked she crooned a song:

"Ships upon the ocean wait;
I must hurry, hurry on!
Mills are idle if I'm late;
I must hurry, hurry on!"

When she reached the Green Meadows Old Mother West Wind opened her bag, turned it upside down and shook it. Out tumbled all the Merry Little Breezes and began to spin round and round for very joy, for you see they were to play in the Green Meadows all day long until Old Mother West Wind should come back at night and take them all to their home behind the Purple Hills.

First they raced over to see Johnny Chuck. They found Johnny Chuck sitting just outside his door eating his breakfast. One, for very mischief, snatched right out of Johnny Chuck's mouth the green leaf of corn he was eating, and ran away with it. Another playfully pulled his whiskers, while a third rumpled up his hair.

Johnny Chuck pretended to be very cross indeed, but really he didn't mind a bit, for Johnny Chuck loved the Merry Little Breezes and played with them every day.

And if they teased Johnny Chuck they were good to him, too. When they saw Farmer Brown coming across the Green Meadows with a gun one of them would dance over to Johnny Chuck and whisper to him that Farmer Brown was coming, and then Johnny Chuck would hide away, deep down in his snug little house under ground, and Farmer Brown would wonder and wonder why it was that he never, never could get near enough to shoot Johnny Chuck. But he never, never could.

When the Merry Little Breezes left Johnny Chuck they raced across the

Green Meadows to the Smiling Pool to say good morning to Grandfather Frog, who sat on a big lily pad watching for green flies for breakfast.

"Chug-arum," said Grandfather Frog, which was his way of saying good morning.

Just then along came a fat green fly and up jumped Grandfather Frog. When he sat down again on the lily pad the fat green fly was nowhere to be seen, but Grandfather Frog looked very well satisfied indeed as he contentedly rubbed his white waistcoat with one hand.

"What is the news, Grandfather Frog?" cried the Merry Little Breezes.

"Mrs. Redwing has a new speckled egg in her nest in the bulrushes," said Grandfather Frog.

"We must see it," cried the Merry Little Breezes, and away they all ran to the swamp where the bulrushes grow.

Now some one else had heard of Mrs. Redwing's dear little nest in the bulrushes, and he had started out bright and early that morning to try and find it, for he wanted to steal the little speckled eggs just because they were pretty. It was Tommy Brown, the farmer's boy.

When the Merry Little Breezes reached the swamp where the bulrushes grow they found poor Mrs. Redwing in great distress. She was afraid that Tommy Brown would find her dear little nest, for he was very, very near it, and his eyes were very, very sharp.

"Oh," cried the Merry Little Breezes, "we must help Mrs. Redwing save her pretty speckled eggs from bad Tommy Brown!"

So one of the Merry Little Breezes whisked Tommy Brown's old straw hat off his head over into the Green Meadows. Of course Tommy ran after it. Just as he stooped to pick it up another little Breeze ran away with it. Then they took turns, first one little Breeze, then another little Breeze running away with the old straw hat just as Tommy Brown would almost get his hands on it. Down past the Smiling Pool and across the Laughing Brook they raced and chased the old straw hat, Tommy Brown running after it, very cross, very red in the face, and breathing very hard. Way across the Green Meadows they ran to the edge of the wood, where they hung the old straw hat in the middle of a thorn tree. By the time Tommy Brown had it once more on his head he had forgotten all about Mrs. Redwing and her dear little nest. Besides, he heard the breakfast horn blowing just then, so off he started for home up the Lone Little Path through the wood.

And all the Merry Little Breezes

danced away across the Green Meadows to the swamp where the bulrushes grow to see the new speckled egg in the dear little nest where Mrs. Redwing was singing for joy. And while she sang the Merry Little Breezes danced among the bulrushes, for they knew, and Mrs. Redwing knew, that some day out of that pretty new speckled egg would come a wee baby Redwing.

II

WHY GRANDFATHER FROG HAS NO TAIL

II

OLD MOTHER WEST WIND had gone to her day's work, leaving all the Merry Little Breezes to play in the Green Meadows. They had played tag and run races with the Bees and played hide and seek with the Sun Beams, and now they had gathered around the Smiling Pool where on a green lily pad sat Grandfather Frog.

Grandfather Frog was old, very old, indeed, and very, very wise. He wore a green coat and his voice was very deep. When Grandfather Frog spoke everybody listened very respectfully. Even Billy Mink treated Grandfather Frog with respect, for Billy Mink's father and his father's father could not remember when Grandfather Frog had not sat on the lily pad watching for green flies.

Down in the Smiling Pool were some of Grandfather Frog's great-great-great-great-great-grandchildren. You wouldn't have known that they were his grandchildren unless some one told you. They didn't look the least bit like Grandfather Frog. They were round and fat and had long tails and perhaps this is why they were called Pollywogs.

"Oh Grandfather Frog, tell us why you don't have a tail as you did when you were young," begged one of the Merry Little Breezes.

Grandfather Frog snapped up a foolish green fly and settled himself on his big lily pad, while all the Merry Little Breezes gathered round to listen.

"Once on a time," began Grandfather Frog, "the Frogs ruled the world, which was mostly water. There was very little dry land — oh, very little indeed! There were no boys to throw stones and no hungry Mink to gobble up foolish Frog-babies who were taking a sun bath!"

Billy Mink, who had joined the Merry Little Breezes and was listening, squirmed uneasily and looked away guiltily.

"In those days all the Frogs had tails, long handsome tails of which they were very, very proud indeed," continued Grandfather Frog. "The King of all the Frogs was twice as big as any other Frog, and his tail was three times as long. He was very proud, oh, very proud indeed of his long tail. He used to sit and admire it until he thought that there never had been and never could be another such tail. He used to wave it back and forth in the water, and every time he waved it all the other Frogs would cry 'Ah!' and 'Oh!' Every day the King grew more vain. He did nothing at all but eat and sleep and admire his tail.

"Now all the other Frogs did just as the King did, so pretty soon none of the Frogs were doing anything but sitting about eating, sleeping and admiring their own tails and the King's.

"Now you all know that people who do nothing worth while in this world are of no use and there is little room for them. So when Mother Nature saw how useless had become the Frog tribe she called the King Frog before her and she said:

"'Because you can think of nothing but your beautiful tail it shall be taken away from you. Because you do nothing but eat and sleep your mouth shall become wide like a door, and your eyes shall start forth from your head. You shall become bow-legged and ugly to look at, and all the world shall laugh at you.'

"The King Frog looked at his beautiful tail and already it seemed to have grown shorter. He looked again and it was shorter still. Every time he looked his tail had grown shorter and smaller. By and by when he looked there was nothing left but a little stub which he couldn't even wriggle. Then even that disappeared, his eyes popped out of his head and his mouth grew bigger and bigger."

Old Grandfather Frog stopped and looked sadly at a foolish green fly coming his way. "Chug-arum," said Grandfather Frog, opening his mouth very wide and hopping up in the air. When he sat down again on his big lily pad the green fly was nowhere to be seen. Grandfather Frog smacked his lips and continued:

"And from that day to this every Frog has started life with a big tail, and as he has grown bigger and bigger his tail has grown smaller and smaller, until finally it disappears, and then he remembers how foolish and useless it is to be vain of what nature has given us. And that is how I came to lose my tail," finished Grandfather Frog.

"Thank you," shouted all the Merry Little Breezes. " We won't forget."

Then they ran a race to see who could reach Johnny Chuck's home first and tell him that Farmer Brown was coming down on the Green Meadows with a gun.

III

HOW REDDY FOX WAS SURPRISED

III

HOW REDDY FOX WAS SURPRISED

JOHNNY CHUCK and Reddy Fox lived very near together on the edge of the Green Meadows. Johnny Chuck was fat and roly-poly. Reddy Fox was slim and wore a bright red coat. Reddy Fox used to like to frighten Johnny Chuck by suddenly popping out from behind a tree and making believe that he was going to eat Johnny Chuck all up.

One bright summer day Johnny Chuck was out looking for a good breakfast of nice tender clover. He had wandered quite a long way from his snug little house in the long meadow grass, although his mother had told him never to go out of sight of the door. But Johnny was like some little boys I know, and forgot all he had been told.

He walked and walked and walked. Every few minutes Johnny Chuck saw something farther on that looked like a patch of nice fresh clover. And every time when he reached it Johnny Chuck found that he had made a mistake. So Johnny Chuck walked and walked and walked.

Old Mother West Wind, coming across the Green Meadows, saw Johnny Chuck and asked him where he was going. Johnny Chuck pretended not to hear and just walked faster.

One of the Merry Little Breezes danced along in front of him.

"Look out, Johnny Chuck; you will get lost," cried the Merry Little Breeze then pulled Johnny's whiskers and ran away.

Higher and higher up in the sky climbed round, red Mr. Sun. Every time Johnny Chuck looked up at him Mr. Sun winked.

"So long as I can see great round, red Mr. Sun and he winks at me I can't be lost," thought Johnny Chuck, and trotted on looking for clover.

By and by Johnny Chuck really did find some clover— just the sweetest clover that grew in the Green Meadows. Johnny Chuck ate and ate and ate and then what do you think he did? Why, he curled right up in the nice sweet clover and went fast asleep.

Great round, red Mr. Sun kept climbing higher and higher up in the sky, then by and by he began to do down on the other side, and long shadows began to creep out across the Green Meadows. Johnny Chuck didn't know anything about them: he was fast asleep.

By and by one of the Merry Little Breezes found Johnny Chuck all curled up in a funny round ball.

"Wake up Johnny Chuck! Wake up!" shouted the Merry Little Breeze.

Johnny Chuck opened his eyes. Then he sat up and rubbed them. For just a few, few minutes he couldn't remember where he was at all.

By and by he sat up very straight to look over the grass and see where he was. But he was so far from home that he didn't see a single thing which looked at all like the things he was used to. The trees were all different. The bushes were all different. Everything was different. Johnny Chuck was lost.

Now, when Johnny sat up, Reddy Fox happened to be looking over the Green Meadows and he saw Johnny's head when it popped above the grass.

"Aha!" said Reddy Fox, "I'll scare

Johnny Chuck so he'll wish he'd never put his nose out of his house."

Then Reddy dropped down behind the long grass and crept softly, oh, ever so softly, through little paths of his own, until he was right behind Johnny Chuck. Johnny Chuck had been so intent looking for home that he didn't see anything else.

Reddy Fox stole right up behind Johnny and pulled Johnny's little short tail hard. How it did frighten Johnny Chuck! He jumped right straight up in the air and when he came down he was the maddest little woodchuck that ever lived in the Green Meadows.

Reddy Fox had thought that Johnny would run, and then Reddy meant to run after him and pull his tail and tease him all the way home. Now, Reddy Fox got as big a surprise as Johnny had had when Reddy pulled his tail. Johnny didn't stop to think that Reddy Fox was twice as big as he, but with his eyes snapping, and chattering as only a little Chuck can chatter, with every little hair on his little body standing right up on end, so that he seemed twice as big as he really was, he started for Reddy Fox.

It surprised Reddy Fox so that he didn't know what to do, and he simply ran. Johnny Chuck ran after him, nipping Reddy's heels every minute or two. Peter Rabbit just happened to be down that way. He was sitting up very straight looking to see what mischief he could get into when he caught sight of Reddy Fox running as hard as ever he could. "It must be that Bowser, the hound, is after Reddy Fox," said Peter Rabbit to himself. "I must watch out that he don't find me."

Just then he caught sight of Johnny Chuck with every little hair standing up on end and running after Reddy Fox as fast as his short legs could go.

"Ho! ho! ho!" shouted Peter Rabbit. "Reddy Fox afraid of Johnny Chuck! Ho! ho! ho!"

Then Peter Rabbit scampered away to find Jimmy Skunk and Bobby Coon and Happy Jack Squirrel to tell them all about how Reddy Fox had run away from Johnny Chuck, for you see they were all a little afraid of Reddy Fox.

Straight home ran Reddy Fox as fast as he could go, and going home he passed the house of Johnny Chuck. Now Johnny couldn't run so fast as Reddy Fox and he was puffing and blowing as only a fat little woodchuck can puff and blow when he has to run hard. Moreover, he had lost his ill temper now and he thought it was the best joke ever was to think that he had actually frightened Reddy Fox. When he came to his own house he stopped and sat on his hind legs once more. Then he shrilled out after Reddy Fox: "Reddy Fox is a 'fraid-cat, 'fraid-cat! Reddy Fox is a 'fraid-cat!"

And all the Merry Little Breezes of Old Mother West Wind, who were playing on the Green Meadows, shouted: "Reddy Fox is a 'fraid-cat, 'fraid-cat!"

And this is the way that Reddy Fox was surprised and that Johnny Chuck found his way home.

IV

WHY JIMMY SKUNK WEARS STRIPES

IV

JIMMY SKUNK, as everybody knows, wears a striped suit, a suit of black and white. There was a time, long, long ago, when all the Skunk family wore black. Very handsome their coats were, too, a beautiful, glossy black. They were very, very proud of them and took the greatest care of them, brushing them carefully ever so many times a day.

There was a Jimmy Skunk then, just as there is now, and he was head of all the Skunk family. Now this Jimmy Skunk was very proud and thought himself very much of a gentleman. He was very independent and cared for no one. Like a great many other independent people, he did not always consider the rights of others. Indeed, it was hinted in the wood and on the Green Meadows that not all of Jimmy Skunk's doings would bear the light of day. It was openly said that he was altogether too fond of prowling about at night, but no one could prove that he was responsible for mischief done in the night, for no one saw him. You see his coat was so black that in the darkness of the night it was not visible at all.

Now about this time of which I am telling you Mrs. Ruffed Grouse made a nest at the foot of the Great Pine and in it she laid fifteen beautiful buff eggs. Mrs. Grouse was very happy, very happy indeed, and all the little meadow folks who knew of her happiness were happy too, for they all loved shy, demure, little Mrs. Grouse. Every morning when Peter Rabbit trotted down the Lone Little Path through the wood past the Great Pine he would stop for a few minutes to chat with Mrs. Grouse. Happy Jack Squirrel would bring her the news every afternoon. The Merry Little Breezes of Old Mother West Wind would run up a dozen times a day to see how she was getting along.

One morning Peter Rabbit, coming down the Lone Little Path for his usual morning call, found a terrible state of affairs. Poor little Mrs. Grouse was heart-broken. All about the foot of the Great Pine lay the empty shells of her beautiful eggs. They had been broken and scattered this way and that.

"How did it happen?" asked Peter Rabbit.

"I don't know," sobbed poor little Mrs. Grouse. "In the night when I was fast asleep something pounced upon me. I managed to get away and fly up in the top of the Great Pine. In the morning I found all my eggs broken, just as you see them here."

Peter Rabbit looked the ground over very carefully. He hunted around behind the Great Pine, he looked under the bushes, he studied the ground with a very wise air. Then he hopped off down the Lone Little Path to the Green Meadows. He stopped at the house of Johnny Chuck.

"What makes your eyes so big and round?" asked Johnny Chuck.

Peter Rabbit came very close so as to whisper in Johnny Chuck's ear, and told him all that he had seen. Together they went to Jimmy Skunk's house. Jimmy Skunk was in bed. He was very sleepy and very cross when he came to the door. Peter Rabbit told him what he had seen.

"Too bad! Too bad!" said Jimmy Skunk, and yawned sleepily.

"Won't you join us in trying to find out who did it?" asked Johnny Chuck.

Jimmy Skunk said he would be delighted to come but that he had some other business that morning and that he would join them in the afternoon. Peter Rabbit and Johnny Chuck went on. Pretty soon they met the Merry Little Breezes and told them the dreadful story.

"What shall we do?" asked Johnny Chuck.

"We'll hurry over and tell Old Dame Nature," cried the Merry Little Breezes, "and ask her what to do."

So away flew the Merry Little Breezes to Old Dame Nature and told her all the dreadful story. Old Dame Nature listened very attentively. Then she sent the Merry Little Breezes to all the little meadow folks to tell every one to be at the Great Pine that afternoon. Now whatever Old Dame Nature commanded

all the little meadow folks were obliged
to do. They did not dare to disobey her.
Promptly at four o'clock that afternoon
all the little meadow folks were gathered
around the foot of the Great Pine.
Broken-hearted Little Mrs. Ruffed Grouse
sat beside her empty nest, with all the
broken shells about her.

Reddy Fox, Peter Rabbit, Johnny
Chuck, Billy Mink, Little Joe Otter,
Jerry Muskrat, Hooty the Owl, Bobby
Coon, Sammy Jay, Blacky the Crow,
Grandfather Frog, Mr. Toad, Spotty the
Turtle, the Merry Little Breezes, all were
there. Last of all came Jimmy Skunk.
Very handsome he looked in his shining
black coat and very sorry he appeared
that such a dreadful thing should have
happened. He told Mrs. Grouse how
badly he felt, and he loudly demanded
that the culprit should be found out and
severely punished.

Old Dame Nature has the most smiling face in the world, but this time it was very, very grave indeed. First she asked little Mrs. Grouse to tell her story all over again that all might hear. Then each in turn was asked to tell where he had been the night before. Johnny Chuck, Happy Jack Squirrel, Striped Chipmunk, Sammy Jay and Blacky the Crow had gone to bed when Mr. Sun went down behind the Purple Hills. Jerry Muskrat, Billy Mink, Little Joe Otter, Grandfather Frog and Spotty the Turtle had not left the Smiling Pool. Bobby Coon had been down in Farmer Brown's cornfield. Hooty the Owl had been hunting in the lower end of the Green Meadows. Peter Rabbit had been down in the berry patch. Mr. Toad had been under the big piece of bark which he called a house. Old Dame Nature called on Jimmy Skunk last of all. Jimmy protested that he had been very, very tired and had gone to bed very early indeed, and had slept the whole night through.

Then Old Dame Nature asked Peter Rabbit what he had found among the egg shells that morning.

Peter Rabbit hopped out and laid three long black hairs before Old Dame Nature. "These," said Peter Rabbit, "are what I found among the egg shells."

Then Old Dame Nature called Johnny Chuck. "Tell us, Johnny Chuck," said she, "what you saw when you called at Jimmy Skunk's house this morning."

"I saw Jimmy Skunk," said Johnny Chuck, "and Jimmy seemed very, very sleepy. It seemed to me that his whiskers were yellow."

"That will do," said Old Dame Nature, and then she called Old Mother West Wind.

"What time did you come down on the

Green Meadows this morning?" asked Old Dame Nature.

"Just at the break of day," said Old Mother West Wind, "as Mr. Sun was coming up from behind the Purple Hills."

"And whom did you see so early in the morning?" asked Old Dame Nature.

"I saw Bobby Coon going home from old Farmer Brown's cornfield," said Old Mother West Wind. "I saw Hooty the Owl coming back from the lower end of the Green Meadows. I saw Peter Rabbit down in the berry patch. Last of all I saw something like a black shadow coming down the Lone Little Path toward the house of Jimmy Skunk."

Every one was looking very hard at Jimmy Skunk. Jimmy began to look very unhappy and very uneasy.

"Who wears a black coat?" asked Dame Nature.

"Jimmy Skunk!" shouted all the little meadow folks.

"What *might* make whiskers yellow?" asked Old Dame Nature.

No one seemed to know at first. Then Peter Rabbit spoke up. "It *might* be the yolk of an egg," said Peter Rabbit.

"Who are likely to be sleepy on a bright sunny morning?" asked Old Dame Nature.

"People who have been out all night," said Johnny Chuck, who himself always goes to bed with the sun.

"Jimmy Skunk," said Old Dame Nature, and her voice was very stern, very stern indeed, and her face was very grave, "Jimmy Skunk, I accuse you of having broken and eaten the eggs of Mrs. Grouse. What have you to say for yourself?"

Jimmy Skunk hung his head. He hadn't a word to say. He just wanted to sneak away by himself.

"Jimmy Skunk," said Old Dame Nature, "because your handsome black coat of which you are so proud has made it possible for you to move about in the night without being seen, and because we can no longer trust you upon your honor, henceforth you and your descendants shall wear a striped coat, which is the sign that you cannot be trusted. Your coat hereafter shall be black and white, that when you move about in the night you will always be visible."

And this is why that to this day Jimmy Skunk wears a striped suit of black and white.

V

THE WILFUL LITTLE BREEZE

V

THE WILFUL LITTLE BREEZE

OLD MOTHER WEST WIND was tired — tired and just a wee bit cross — cross because she was tired. She had had a very busy day. Ever since early morning she had been puffing out the white sails of the ships on the big ocean that they might go faster; she had kept all the big and little wind mills whirling and whirling to pump water for thirsty folks and grind corn for hungry folks; she had blown away all the smoke from tall chimneys and engines and steamboats. Yes, indeed, Old Mother West Wind had been very, very busy.

Now she was coming across the Green

Meadows on her way to her home behind the Purple Hills, and as she came she opened the big bag she carried and called to her children, the Merry Little Breezes, who had been playing hard on the Green Meadows all the long day. One by one they crept into the big bag, for they were tired, too, and ready to go to their home behind the Purple Hills.

Pretty soon all were in the bag but one, a wilful little Breeze, who was not quite ready to go home; he wanted to play just a little longer. He danced ahead of Old Mother West Wind. He kissed the sleepy daisies. He shook the nodding buttercups. He set all the little poplar leaves a dancing, too, and he wouldn't come into the big bag.

So Old Mother West Wind closed the big bag and slung it over her shoulder. Then she started on towards her home behind the Purple Hills.

When she had gone the wilful little Breeze left behind suddenly felt very lonely — very lonely indeed! The sleepy daisies didn't want to play. The nodding buttercups were cross. Great round bright Mr. Sun, who had been shining and shining all day long, went to bed and put on his night cap of golden clouds. Black shadows came creeping, creeping out into the Green Meadows.

The wilful little Breeze began to wish that he was safe in Old Mother West Wind's big bag with all the other Merry Little Breezes.

So he started across the Green Meadows to find the Purple Hills. But all the hills were black now and he could not tell which he should look behind to find his home with Old Mother West Wind and the Merry Little Breezes. How he did wish that he had minded Old Mother West Wind.

By and by he curled up under a bayberry bush and tried to go to sleep, but
he was lonely, oh, so lonely! and he
couldn't go to sleep. Old Mother Moon
came up and flooded all the Green Meadows with light, but it wasn't like the
bright light of jolly round Mr. Sun, for it
was cold and white and it made many
black shadows.

Pretty soon the wilful little Breeze
heard Hooty the Owl out hunting for
a meadow mouse for his dinner. Then
down the Lone Little Path which ran
close to the bayberry bush trotted Reddy
Fox. He was trotting very softly and
every minute or so he turned his
head and looked behind him to see if
he was followed. It was plain to
see that Reddy Fox was bent on mischief.

When he reached the bayberry bush
Reddy Fox sat down and barked twice.

Hooty the Owl answered him at once and flew over to join him. They didn't see the wilful little Breeze curled up under the bayberry bush, so intent were these two rogues in plotting mischief. They were planning to steal down across the Green Meadows to the edge of the Brown Pasture where Mr. Bob White and pretty Mrs. Bob White and a dozen little Bob Whites had their home.

"When they run along the ground I'll catch 'em, and when they fly up in the air you'll catch 'em and we'll gobble 'em all up," said Reddy Fox to Hooty the Owl. Then he licked his chops and Hooty the Owl snapped his bill, just as if they were tasting tender little Bob Whites that very minute. It made the wilful little Breeze shiver to see them. Pretty soon they started on towards the Brown Pasture.

When they were out of sight the wilful

little Breeze jumped up and shook himself. Then away he sped across the Green Meadows to the Brown Pasture. And because he could go faster and because he went a shorter way he got there first. He had to hunt and hunt to find Mrs. and Mr. Bob White and all the little Bob Whites, but finally he did find them, all with their heads tucked under their wings fast asleep.

The wilful little Breeze shook Mr. Bob White very gently. In an instant he was wide awake.

"Sh-h-h," said the wilful little Breeze. "Reddy Fox and Hooty the Owl are coming to the Brown Pasture to gobble up you and Mrs. Bob White and all the little Bob Whites."

"Thank you, little Breeze," said Mr. Bob White, "I think I'll move my family."

Then he woke Mrs. Bob White and all

the little Bob Whites. With Mr. Bob
White in the lead away they all flew to
the far side of the Brown Pasture where
they were soon safely hidden under a
juniper tree.

The wilful little Breeze saw them safely
there, and when they were nicely hidden
hurried back to the place where the Bob
Whites had been sleeping. Reddy Fox
was stealing up through the grass very,
very softly. Hooty the Owl was flying
as silently as a shadow. When Reddy
Fox thought he was near enough he drew
himself together, made a quick spring
and landed right in Mr. Bob White's
empty bed. Reddy Fox and Hooty the
Owl looked so surprised and foolish when
they found that the Bob Whites were not
there that the wilful little Breeze nearly
laughed out loud.

Then Reddy Fox and Hooty the Owl
hunted here and hunted there, all over

the Brown Pasture, but they couldn't find
the Bob Whites.

And the wilful little Breeze went back
to the juniper tree and curled himself up
beside Mr. Bob White to sleep, for he
was lonely no longer.

VI

REDDY FOX GOES FISHING

VI

REDDY FOX GOES FISHING

ONE morning when Mr. Sun was very, very bright and it was very, very warm, down on the Green Meadows Reddy Fox came hopping and skipping down the Lone Little Path that leads to the Laughing Brook. Hoppity, skip, skippity hop! Reddy felt very much pleased with himself that sunny morning. Pretty soon he saw Johnny Chuck sitting up very straight close by the little house where he lives.

"Johnny Chuck, Chuck, Chuck! Johnny Chuck, Chuck, Chuck! Johnny Woodchuck!" called Reddy Fox.

Johnny Chuck pretended not to hear. His mother had told him not to play with

Reddy Fox, for Reddy Fox was a bad boy.

"Johnny Chuck, Chuck, Chuck! Johnny Woodchuck!" called Reddy again.

This time Johnny turned and looked. He could see Reddy Fox turning somersaults and chasing his tail and rolling over and over in the little path.

"Come on!" said Reddy Fox. "Let's go fishing!"

"Can't," said Johnny Chuck, because, you know, his mother had told him not to play with Reddy Fox.

"I'll show you how to catch a fish," said Reddy Fox, and tried to jump over his own shadow.

"Can't," said good little Johnny Chuck again, and turned away so that he couldn't see Reddy Fox chasing Butterflies and playing catch with the Field Mice children.

So Reddy Fox went down to the Laughing Brook all alone. The Brook was laughing and singing on its way to join the Big River. The sky was blue and the sun was bright. Reddy Fox jumped on the Big Rock in the middle of the Laughing Brook and peeped over the other side. What do you think he saw? Why, right down below in a Dear Little Pool were Mr. and Mrs. Trout and all the little Trouts.

Reddy Fox wanted some of those little Trouts to take home for his dinner, but he didn't know how to catch them. He lay flat down on the Big Rock and reached way down into the Dear Little Pool, but all the little Trouts laughed at Reddy Fox and not one came within reach. Then Mr. Trout swam up so quickly that Reddy Fox didn't see him coming and bit Reddy's little black paw hard.

"Ouch!" cried Reddy Fox, pulling

his little black paw out of the water.
And all the little Trouts laughed at
Reddy Fox.

Just then along came Billy Mink.

"Hello, Reddy Fox!" said Billy Mink.
"What are you doing here?"

"I'm trying to catch a fish," said
Reddy Fox.

"Pooh! That's easy!" said Billy
Mink. "I'll show you how."

So Billy Mink lay down on the Big
Rock side of Reddy Fox and peeped over
into the Dear Little Pool where all the
little Trouts were laughing at Reddy Fox
and having such a good time. But Billy
Mink took care, such very great care,
that Mr. Trout and Mrs. Trout should not
see him peeping over into the Dear Little
Pool.

When Billy Mink saw all those little
Trouts playing in the Dear Little Pool
he laughed. "You count three, Reddy

Fox," said he, "and I'll show you how to catch a fish."

"One!" said Reddy Fox, "Two! Three!"

Splash! Billy Mink had dived head first into the Dear Little Pool. He spattered water way up onto Reddy Fox, and he frightened old Mr. Frog so that he fell over backwards off the lily pad where he was taking a morning nap right into the water. In a minute Billy Mink climbed out on the other side of the Dear Little Pool and sure enough, he had caught one of the little Trouts.

"Give it to me," cried Reddy Fox.

"Catch one yourself," said Billy Mink. "Old Grandpa Mink wants a fish for his dinner, so I'm going to take this home. You're afraid, Reddy Fox! 'Fraid-cat! Fraid-cat!"

Billy Mink shook the water off of his

little brown coat, picked up the little Trout and ran off home.

Reddy Fox lay down again on the Big Rock and peeped into the Dear Little Pool. Not a single Trout could he see. They were all hiding safely with Mr. and Mrs. Trout. Reddy Fox watched and watched. The sun was warm, the Langhing Brook was singing a lullaby and — what do you think? Why, Reddy Fox went fast asleep right on the edge of the great Big Rock.

By and by Reddy Fox began to dream. He dreamed that he had a nice little brown coat that was waterproof, just like the little brown coat that Billy Mink wore. Yes, and he dreamed that he had learned to swim and to catch fish just as Billy Mink did. He dreamed that the Dear Little Pool was full of little Trouts and that he was just going to catch one when — splash! Reddy Fox had rolled right off of the Big Rock into the Dear Little Pool.

The water went into the eyes of Reddy Fox, and it went up his nose and he swallowed so much that he felt as if he never, never would want another drink of water. And his beautiful red coat, which old Mother Fox had told him to be very, very careful of because he couldn't have another for a whole year, was oh so wet! And his pants were wet and his beautiful bushy tail, of which he was so proud, was so full of water that he couldn't hold it up, but had to drag it up the bank after him as he crawled out of the Dear Little Pool.

"Ha! Ha! Ha!" laughed Mr. Kingfisher, sitting on a tree.

"Ho! Ho! Ho!" laughed old Mr. Frog, who had climbed back on his lily pad.

"He! He! He!" laughed all the

little Trouts and Mr. Trout and Mrs. Trout, swimming round and round in the Dear Little Pool.

"Ha! Ha! Ha! Ho! Ho! Ho! He! He! He!" laughed Billy Mink, who had come back to the Big Rock just in time to see Reddy Fox tumble in.

Reddy Fox didn't say a word, he was so ashamed. He just crept up the Lone Little Path to his home, dragging his tail, all wet and muddy, behind him, and dripping water all the way.

Johnny Chuck was still sitting by his door as his mother had told him to. Reddy Fox tried to go past without being seen, but Johnny Chuck's bright little eyes saw him.

"Where are your fish, Reddy Fox?" called Johnny Chuck.

Reddy Fox said never a word, but walked faster.

"Why don't you turn somersaults,

and jump over your shadow and chase Butterflies and play with the little Field Mice, Reddy Fox?" called Johnny Chuck.

But Reddy Fox just walked faster. When he got most home he saw old Mother Fox sitting in the doorway with a great big switch across her lap, for Mother Fox had told Reddy Fox not to go near the Laughing Brook.

And this is all I am going to tell you about how Reddy Fox went fishing.

VII

JIMMY SKUNK LOOKS FOR BEETLES

JIMMY SKUNK LOOKS FOR BEETLES

JIMMY SKUNK opened his eyes very early one morning and peeped out of his snug little house on the hill. Big, round Mr. Sun, with a very red, smiling face, had just begun to climb up into the sky. Old Mother West Wind was just starting down to the Green Meadows with her big bag over her shoulder. In that bag Jimmy Skunk knew she carried all her children, the Merry Little Breezes, whom she was taking down to the Green Meadows to play and frolic all day.

"Good morning, Mother West Wind," said Jimmy Skunk, politely. "Did you see any beetles as you came down the hill?"

Old Mother West Wind said, no, she hadn't seen any beetles as she came down the hill.

"Thank you," said Jimmy Skunk, politely. "I guess I'll have to go look myself, for I'm very, very hungry."

So Jimmy Skunk brushed his handsome black and white coat, and washed his face and hands, and started out to try to find some beetles for his breakfast. First he went down to the Green Meadows and stopped at Johnny Chuck's house. But Johnny Chuck was still in bed and fast asleep. Then Jimmy Skunk went over to see if Reddy Fox would go with him to help find some beetles for his breakfast. But Reddy Fox had been out very, very late the night before and he was still in bed fast asleep, too.

So Jimmy Skunk set out all alone along

the Crooked Little Path up the hill to find some beetles for his breakfast. He walked very slowly, for Jimmy Skunk never hurries. He stopped and peeped under every old log to see if there were any beetles. By and by he came to a big piece of bark beside the Crooked Little Path. Jimmy Skunk took hold of the piece of bark with his two little black paws and pulled and pulled. All of a sudden, the big piece of bark turned over so quickly that Jimmy Skunk fell flat on his back.

When Jimmy Skunk had rolled over onto his feet again, there sat old Mr. Toad right in the path, and old Mr. Toad was very, very cross indeed. He swelled and he puffed and he puffed and he swelled, till he was twice as big as Jimmy Skunk had ever seen him before.

"Good morning, Mr. Toad," said

Jimmy Skunk. "Have you seen any beetles?"

But Mr. Toad blinked his great round goggly eyes and he said:

"What do you mean, Jimmy Skunk, by pulling the roof off my house?"

"Is that the roof of your house?" asked Jimmy Skunk politely. "I won't do it again."

Then Jimmy Skunk stepped right over old Mr. Toad, and went on up the Crooked Little Path to look for some beetles.

By and by he came to an old stump of a tree which was hollow and had the nicest little round hole in one side. Jimmy Skunk took hold of one edge with his two little black paws and pulled and pulled. All of a sudden the whole side of the old stump tore open and Jimmy Skunk fell flat on his back.

When Jimmy Skunk had rolled over

onto his feet again there was Striped Chipmunk hopping up and down right in the middle of the path, he was so angry.

"Good morning, Striped Chipmunk," said Jimmy Skunk. "Have you seen any beetles?"

But Striped Chipmunk hopped faster than ever and he said:

"What do you mean, Jimmy Skunk, by pulling the side off my house?"

"Is that the side of your house?" asked Jimmy Skunk, politely. "I won't do it again."

Then Jimmy Skunk stepped right over Striped Chipmunk, and went on up the Crooked Little Path to look for some beetles.

Pretty soon he met Peter Rabbit hopping along down the Crooked Little Path. "Good morning, Jimmy Skunk, where are you going so early in the morning?" said Peter Rabbit.

"Good morning, Peter Rabbit. Have you seen any beetles?" asked Jimmy Skunk, politely.

"No, I haven't seen any beetles, but I'll help you find some," said Peter Rabbit. So he turned about and hopped ahead of Jimmy Skunk up the Crooked Little Path.

Now because Peter Rabbit's legs are long and he is always in a hurry, he got to the top of the hill first. When Jimmy Skunk reached the end of the Crooked Little Path on the top of the hill he found Peter Rabbit sitting up very straight and looking and looking very hard at a great flat stone.

"What are you looking at, Peter Rabbit?" asked Jimmy Skunk.

"Sh-h-h!" said Peter Rabbit, "I think there are some beetles under that great flat stone where that little black string is sticking out. Now when I count three you grab that string and pull hard; perhaps you'll find a beetle at the other end."

So Jimmy Skunk got ready and Peter Rabbit began to count.

"One!" said Peter. "Two!" said Peter. "Three!"

Jimmy Skunk grabbed the black string and pulled as hard as ever he could and out came — Mr. Black Snake! The string Jimmy Skunk had pulled was Mr. Black Snake's tail, and Mr. Black Snake was very, very angry indeed.

"Ha! Ha! Ha!" laughed Peter Rabbit.

"What do you mean, Jimmy Skunk," said Mr. Black Snake, "by pulling my tail?"

"Was that your tail?" said Jimmy Skunk, politely. "I won't do it again. Have you seen any beetles?"

But Mr. Black Snake hadn't seen any

beetles and he was so cross that Jimmy Skunk went on over the hill to look for some beetles.

Peter Rabbit was still laughing and laughing and laughing. And the more he laughed the angrier grew Mr. Black Snake, till finally he started after Peter Rabbit to teach him a lesson.

Then Peter Rabbit stopped laughing, for Mr. Black Snake can run very fast. Away went Peter Rabbit down the Crooked Little Path as fast as he could go, and away went Mr. Black Snake after him.

But Jimmy Skunk didn't even look once to see if Mr. Black Snake had caught Peter Rabbit, for Jimmy Skunk had found some beetles and was eating his breakfast.

VIII
BILLY MINK'S SWIMMING PARTY

VIII

BILLY MINK was coming down the bank of the Laughing Brook. Billy Mink was feeling very good indeed. He had had a good breakfast, the sun was warm, little white cloud ships were sailing across the blue sky and their shadows were sailing across the Green Meadows, the birds were singing and the bees were humming. Billy Mink felt like singing too, but Billy Mink's voice was not meant for singing.

By and by Billy Mink came to the Smiling Pool. Here the Laughing Brook stopped and rested on its way to join the Big River. It stopped its noisy laughing and singing and just lay smiling and smiling in the warm sunshine. The little flowers on the bank leaned over and nodded to it. The beech tree, which was very old, sometimes dropped a leaf into it. The cat-tails kept their feet cool in the edge of it.

Billy Mink jumped out on the Big Rock and looked down into the Smiling Pool. Over on a green lily pad he saw old Grandfather Frog.

"Hello, Grandfather Frog," said Billy Mink.

"Hello, Billy Mink," said Grandfather Frog. "What mischief are you up to this fine sunny morning?"

Just then Billy Mink saw a little brown head swimming along one edge of the Smiling Pool.

"Hello, Jerry Muskrat!" shouted Billy Mink.

"Hello your own self, Billy Mink,"

shouted Jerry Muskrat, "Come in and have a swim; the water's fine!"

"Good," said Billy Mink. "We'll have a swimming party."

So Billy Mink called all the Merry Little Breezes of Old Mother West Wind, who were playing with the flowers on the bank, and sent them to find Little Joe Otter and invite him to come to the swimming party. Pretty soon back came the Little Breezes and with them came Little Joe Otter.

"Hello, Billy Mink," said Little Joe Otter. "Here I am!"

"Hello, Little Joe Otter," said Billy Mink. "Come up here on the Big Rock and see who can dive the deepest into the Smiling Pool."

So Little Joe Otter and Jerry Muskrat climbed up on the Big Rock side of Billy Mink and they all stood side by side in their little brown bathing

suits looking down into the Smiling
Pool.

"Now when I count three we'll all
dive into the Smiling Pool together and
see who can dive the deepest. One!"
said Billy Mink. "Two!" said Billy
Mink. "Three!" said Billy Mink.

And when he said "Three" in they
all went head first. My, such a splash as
they did make! They upset old Grandfather Frog so that he fell off his lily pad.
They frightened Mr. and Mrs. Trout so
that they jumped right out of the water.
Tiny Tadpole had such a scare that he hid
way, way down in the mud with only the
tip of his funny little nose sticking out.

"Chug-a-rum," said old Grandfather
Frog, climbing out of his lily pad. "If
I wasn't so old I would show you how to
dive."

"Come on, Grandfather Frog!" cried
Billy Mink. "Show us how to dive."

And what do you think? Why, old Grandfather Frog actually got so excited that he climbed up on the Big Rock to show them how to dive. Splash! went Grandfather Frog into the Smiling Pool. Splash! went Billy Mink right behind him. Splash! Splash! went Little Joe Otter and Jerry Muskrat, right at Billy Mink's heels.

"Hurrah!" shouted Mr. Kingfisher, sitting on a branch of the old beech tree. And then just to show them that he could dive, too, splash! he went into the Smiling Pool.

Such a noise as they did make! All the Little Breezes of Old Mother West Wind danced for joy on the bank. Blacky the Crow and Sammy Jay flew over to see what was going on.

"Now let's see who can swim the farthest under water," cried Billy Mink.

So they all stood side by side on one edge of the Smiling Pool.

"Go!" shouted Mr. Kingfisher, and in they all plunged. Little ripples ran across the Smiling Pool and then the water became as smooth and smiling as if nothing had gone into it with a plunge.

Now old Grandfather Frog began to realize that he wasn't as young as he used to be, and he couldn't swim as fast as the others anyway. He began to get short of breath, so he swam up to the top and stuck just the tip of his nose out to get some more air. Sammy Jay's sharp eyes saw him.

"There's Grandfather Frog!" he shouted.

So then Grandfather Frog popped his head out and swam over to his green lily pad to rest.

Way over beyond the Big Rock little bubbles in three long rows kept coming up to the top of the Smiling Pool. They showed just where Billy Mink, Little Joe Otter and Jerry Muskrat were swimming way down out of sight. It was the air from their lungs making the bubbles. Straight across the Smiling Pool went the lines of little bubbles and then way out on the farther side two little heads bobbed out of water close together. They were Billy Mink and Little Joe Otter. A moment later Jerry Muskrat bobbed up beside them.

You see they had swum clear across the Smiling Pool and of course they could swim no farther.

So Billy Mink's swimming party was a great success.

IX

PETER RABBIT PLAYS A JOKE

PETER RABBIT PLAYS A JOKE

ONE morning when big round Mr. Sun was climbing up in the sky and Old Mother West Wind had sent all her Merry Little Breezes to play in the Green Meadows, Johnny Chuck started out for a walk. First he sat up very straight and looked and looked all around to see if Reddy Fox was anywhere about, for you know Reddy Fox liked to tease Johnny Chuck.

But Reddy Fox was nowhere to be seen, so Johnny Chuck trotted down the Lone Little Path to the wood. Mr. Sun was shining as brightly as ever he could and Johnny Chuck, who was very, very fat, grew very, very warm. By and by he sat down on the end of a log under a big tree to rest.

Thump! Something hit Johnny Chuck right on the top of his round little head. It made Johnny Chuck jump.

"Hello, Johnny Chuck!" said a voice that seemed to come right out of the sky. Johnny Chuck tipped his head way, way back and looked up. He was just in time to see Happy Jack Squirrel drop a nut. Down it came and hit Johnny Chuck right on the tip of his funny, black, little nose.

"Oh!" said Johnny Chuck, and tumbled right over back off the log. But Johnny Chuck was so round and so fat and so roly-poly that it didn't hurt him a bit.

"Ha! Ha! Ha!" laughed Happy Jack up in the tree.

"Ha! Ha! Ha!" laughed Johnny Chuck, picking himself up. Then they both laughed together, it was such a good joke.

"What are you laughing at?" asked a voice so close to Johnny Chuck that he rolled over three times he was so surprised. It was Peter Rabbit.

"What are you doing in my wood?" asked Peter Rabbit.

"I'm taking a walk," said Johnny Chuck.

"Good," said Peter Rabbit, "I'll come along too."

So Johnny Chuck and Peter Rabbit set out along the Lone Little Path through the wood. Peter Rabbit hopped along with great big jumps, for Peter's legs are long and meant for jumping, but Johnny Chuck couldn't keep up though he tried very hard, for Johnny's legs are short. Pretty soon Peter Rabbit came back, walking very softly. He whispered in Johnny Chuck's ear.

"I've found something," said Peter Rabbit.

"What is it?" asked Johnny Chuck.

"I'll show you," said Peter Rabbit, "but you must be very, very still, and not make the least little bit of noise."

Johnny Chuck promised to be very, very still for he wanted very much to see what Peter Rabbit had found. Peter Rabbit tip-toed down the Lone Little Path through the wood, his funny long ears pointing right up to the sky. And behind him tip-toed Johnny Chuck, wondering and wondering what it could be that Peter Rabbit had found.

Pretty soon they came to a nice mossy green log right across the Lone Little Path. Peter Rabbit stopped and sat up very straight. He looked this way and looked that way. Johnny Chuck stopped too and he sat up very straight and looked this way and looked that way, but all he could see was the mossy green log across the Lone Little Path.

"What is it, Peter Rabbit?" whispered Johnny Chuck.

"You can't see it yet," whispered Peter Rabbit, "for first we have to jump over that mossy green log. Now I'll jump first, and then you jump just the way I do, and then you'll see what it is I've found," said Peter Rabbit.

So Peter Rabbit jumped first, and because his legs are long and meant for jumping, he jumped way, way over the mossy green log. Then he turned around and sat up to see Johnny Chuck jump over the mossy green log, too.

Johnny Chuck tried to jump very high and very far, just as he had seen Peter Rabbit jump, but Johnny Chuck's legs are very short and not meant for jumping. Besides, Johnny Chuck was very, very fat. So though he tried very hard indeed to jump just like Peter Rabbit, he stubbed his toes on the top of the mossy green log and over he tumbled, head first, and landed with a great big thump right on Reddy Fox, who was lying fast asleep on the other side of the mossy green log.

Peter Rabbit laughed and laughed until he had to hold his sides.

My, how frightened Johnny Chuck was when he saw what he had done! Before he could get on his feet he had rolled right over behind a little bush, and there he lay very, very still.

Reddy Fox awoke with a grunt when Johnny Chuck fell on him so hard, and the first thing he saw was Peter Rabbit laughing so that he had to hold his sides. Reddy Fox didn't stop to look around. He thought that Peter Rabbit had jumped on him. Up jumped Reddy Fox and away ran Peter Rabbit. Away went Reddy Fox after Peter Rabbit. Peter

The door of the house was too small for Reddy
Fox to squeeze in.

dodged behind the trees, and jumped over the bushes, and ran this way and ran that way, just as hard as ever he could, for Peter Rabbit was very much afraid of Reddy Fox. And Reddy Fox followed Peter Rabbit behind the trees and over the bushes this way and that way, but he couldn't catch Peter Rabbit. Pretty soon Peter Rabbit came to the house of Jimmy Skunk. He knew that Jimmy Skunk was over in the pasture, so he popped right in and then he was safe, for the door of Jimmy Skunk's house was too small for Reddy Fox to squeeze in. Reddy Fox sat down and waited, but Peter Rabbit didn't come out. By and by Reddy Fox gave it up and trotted off home where old Mother Fox was waiting for him.

All this time Johnny Chuck had sat very still, watching Reddy Fox try to catch Peter Rabbit. And when he saw

Peter Rabbit pop into the house of Jimmy Skunk and Reddy Fox trot away home, Johnny Chuck stood up and brushed his little coat very clean and then he trotted back up the Lone Little Path through the wood to his own dear little path through the Green Meadows where the Merry Little Breezes of Old Mother West Wind were still playing, till he was safe in his own snug little home once more.

X

HOW SAMMY JAY WAS FOUND OUT

X

HOW SAMMY JAY WAS FOUND OUT

SAMMY JAY was very busy, very busy indeed. When any one happened that way Sammy Jay pretended to be doing nothing at all, for Sammy Jay thought himself a very fine gentleman. He was very proud of his handsome blue coat with white trimmings and his high cap, and he would sit on a fence post and make fun of Johnny Chuck working at a new door for his snug little home in the Green Meadows, and of Striped Chipmunk storing up heaps of corn and nuts for the winter, for most of the time Sammy Jay was an idle fellow. And when Sammy Jay *was* busy, he was pretty sure to be doing something he ought not to do, for idle people almost always get into mischief.

Sammy Jay was in mischief now, and that is why he pretended to be doing nothing when he thought any one was looking.

Old Mother West Wind had come down from her home behind the Purple Hills very early that morning. Indeed, jolly, round, red Mr. Sun had hardly gotten out of bed when she crossed the Green Meadows on her way to help the big ships across the ocean. Old Mother West Wind's eyes were sharp, and she saw Sammy Jay before Sammy Jay saw her.

"Now what can Sammy Jay be so busy about, and why is he so very, very quiet?" thought Old Mother West Wind. "He must be up to some mischief."

So when she opened her big bag and turned out all her Merry Little Breezes to play on the Green Meadows she sent one of them to see what Sammy Jay was doing in the old chestnut tree. The Merry Little Breeze danced along over the tree tops just as if he hadn't a thought in the world but to wake up all the little leaves and set them to dancing too, and Sammy Jay, watching Old Mother West Wind and the other Merry Little Breezes, didn't see this Merry Little Breeze at all.

Pretty soon it danced back to Old Mother West Wind and whispered in her ear: "Sammy Jay is stealing the nuts Happy Jack Squirrel had hidden in the hollow of the old chestnut tree, and is hiding them for himself in the tumble down nest that Blacky the Crow built in the Great Pine last year." "Aha!" said Old Mother West Wind. Then she went on across the Green Meadows.

"Good morning, Old Mother West

Wind," said Sammy Jay as she passed the fence post where he was sitting.

"Good morning, Sammy Jay," said Old Mother West Wind. "What brings you out so early in the morning?"

"I'm out for my health, Old Mother West Wind," said Sammy Jay politely. "The doctor has ordered me to take a bath in the dew at sunrise every morning."

Old Mother West Wind said nothing, but went on her way across the Green Meadows to blow the ships across the ocean. When she had passed Sammy Jay hurried to take the last of Happy Jack's nuts to the old nest in the Great Pine.

Poor Happy Jack! Soon he came dancing along with another nut to put in the hollow of the old chestnut tree. When he peeped in and saw that all his big store of nuts had disappeared he couldn't believe his own eyes. He put in one paw and felt all around but not a nut could he feel. Then he climbed in and sure enough, the hollow was empty.

Poor Happy Jack! There were tears in his eyes when he crept out again. He looked all around but no one was to be seen but handsome Sammy Jay, very busy brushing his beautiful blue coat.

"Good morning, Sammy Jay, have you seen any one pass this way?" asked Happy Jack. "Some one has stolen my store of nuts from the hollow in the old chestnut tree."

Sammy Jay pretended to feel very badly indeed, and in his sweetest voice, for his voice was very sweet in those days, he offered to help Happy Jack try to catch the thief who had stolen the store of nuts from the hollow in the old chestnut tree.

Together they went down across the

Green Meadows asking every one whom they met if they had seen the thief who had stolen Happy Jack's store of nuts from the hollow in the old chestnut tree. All the Merry Little Breezes joined in the search, and soon every one who lived in the Green Meadows or in the wood knew that some one had stolen all of Happy Jack Squirrel's store of nuts from the hollow in the old chestnut tree. And because every one liked Happy Jack, every one felt very sorry indeed for him.

The next morning all the Merry Little Breezes of Old Mother West Wind were turned out of the big bag into the Green Meadows very early indeed, for they had a lot of errands to do. All over the Green Meadows they hurried, all through the wood, up and down the Laughing Brook and all around the Smiling Pool, inviting everybody to meet at the Great Pine on the hill at nine o'clock to form a committee of the whole — that's what Old Mother West Wind called it — a committee of the whole — to try to find the thief who stole Happy Jack's nuts from the hollow in the old chestnut tree.

And because every one liked Happy Jack every one went to the Great Pine on the hill — Reddy Fox, Bobby Coon, Jimmy Skunk, Striped Chipmunk, who is Happy Jack's cousin you know, Billy Mink, Little Joe Otter, Jerry Muskrat, Hooty the Owl, who was almost too sleepy to keep his eyes open, Blacky the Crow, Johnny Chuck, Peter Rabbit, even old Grandfather Frog. Of course Sammy Jay was there, looking his handsomest.

When they had all gathered around the Great Pine, Old Mother West Wind pointed to the old nest way up in the top of it. "Is that your nest?" she asked Blacky the Crow.

"It was, but I gave it to my cousin, Sammy Jay," said Blacky the Crow.

"Is that your nest, and may I have a stick out of it?" asked Old Mother West Wind of Sammy Jay.

"It is," said Sammy Jay, with his politest bow, "and you are welcome to a stick out of it." To himself he thought, "She will only take one from the top and that won't matter."

Old Mother West Wind suddenly puffed out her cheeks and blew so hard that she blew a big stick right out of the bottom of the old nest. Down it fell bumpity-bump on the branches of the Great Pine After it fell — what do you think? Why, hickory nuts and chestnuts and acorns and hazel nuts, such a lot of them!

"Why! Why-e-e!" cried Happy Jack. "There are all my stolen nuts!"

Everybody turned to look at Sammy Jay, but he was flying off through the wood as fast as he could go. "Stop thief!" cried Old Mother West Wind. "Stop thief!" cried all the Merry Little Breezes and Johnny Chuck and Billy Mink and all the rest. But Sammy Jay didn't stop.

Then all began to pick up the nuts that had fallen from the old nest where Sammy Jay had hidden them. By and by, with Happy Jack leading the way, they all marched back to the old chestnut tree and there Happy Jack stored all the nuts away in his snug little hollow once more.

And ever since that day, Sammy Jay, whenever he tries to call, just screams: "Thief!" "Thief!" "Thief!"

XI

JERRY MUSKRAT'S PARTY

JERRY MUSKRAT'S PARTY

ALL the Merry Little Breezes of Old Mother West Wind were hurrying over the Green Meadows. Some flew this way and some ran that way and some danced the other way. You see Jerry Muskrat had asked them to carry his invitations to a party at the Big Rock in the Smiling Pool.

Of course every one said that they would be delighted to go to Jerry Muskrat's party. Round Mr. Sun shone his very brightest. The sky was its bluest and the little birds had promised to be there to sing for Jerry Muskrat, so of course all the little folks in the Green Meadows and in the wood wanted to go.

There were Johnny Chuck and Reddy Fox and Jimmy Skunk and Bobby Coon and Happy Jack Squirrel and Striped Chipmunk and Billy Mink and Little Joe Otter and Grandfather Frog and old Mr. Toad and Mr. Blacksnake—all going to Jerry Muskrat's party.

When they reached the Smiling Pool they found Jerry Muskrat all ready. His brothers and his sisters, his aunts and his uncles and his cousins were all there. Such a merry, merry time as there was in the Smiling Pool! How the water did splash! Billy Mink and Little Joe Otter and Grandfather Frog jumped right in as soon as they got there. They played tag in the water and hide and seek behind the Big Rock. They turned somersaults down the slippery slide and they had such a good time!

But Reddy Fox and Peter Rabbit and Bobby Coon and Johnny Chuck and Jimmy Skunk and Happy Jack and Striped Chipmunk couldn't swim, so of course they couldn't play tag in the water or hide and seek or go down the slippery slide; all they could do was sit around to look on and wish that they knew how to swim, too. So of course they didn't have a good time. Soon they began to wish that they hadn't come to Jerry Muskrat's party. When he found that they were not having a good time, poor Jerry Muskrat felt very badly indeed. You see he lives in the water so much that he had quite forgotten that there was any one who couldn't swim, or he never, never would have invited all the little meadow folks who live on dry land.

"Let's go home," said Peter Rabbit to Johnny Chuck.

"We can have more fun up on the hill," said Jimmy Skunk.

Just then Little Joe Otter came pushing a great big log across the Smiling Pool.

"Here's a ship, Bobby Coon. You get on one end and I'll give you a sail across the Smiling Pool," shouted Little Joe Otter.

So Bobby Coon crawled out on the big log and held on very tight, while little Joe Otter swam behind and pushed the big log. Across the Smiling Pool they went and back again. Bobby,Coon had such a good ride that he wanted to go again, but Jimmy Skunk wanted a ride. So Bobby Coon hopped off of the big log and Jimmy Skunk hopped on and away he went across the Smiling Pool with little Joe Otter pushing behind.

Then Jerry Muskrat found another log and gave Peter Rabbit a ride. Jerry Muskrat's brothers and sisters and aunts and uncles and cousins found logs and took Reddy Fox and Johnny Chuck and even Mr. Toad back and forth across the Smiling Pool.

Happy Jack Squirrel sat up very straight on the end of his log and spread his great bushy tail for a sail. All the little Breezes blew and blew and Happy Jack Squirrel sailed round and round the Smiling Pool.

Sometimes some one would fall off into the water and get wet, but Jerry Muskrat or Billy Mink always pulled them out again, and no one cared the tiniest bit for a wetting.

In the bushes around the Smiling Pool the little birds sang and sang. Reddy Fox barked his loudest. Happy Jack Squirrel chattered and chir-r-r-ed. All the muskrats squealed and squeaked, for Jerry Muskrat's party was such fun!

By and by when Mr. Sun went down

behind the Purple Hills to his home and
Old Mother West Wind with all her Merry
Little Breezes went after him, and the
little stars came out to twinkle and
twinkle, the Smiling Pool lay all quiet and
still, but smiling and smiling to think
what a good time every one had had at
Jerry Muskrat's party.

XII

BOBBY COON AND REDDY FOX PLAY TRICKS

XII

BOBBY COON AND REDDY FOX PLAY TRICKS

IT was night. All the little stars were looking down and twinkling and twinkling. Mother Moon was doing her best to make the Green Meadows as light as Mr. Sun did in the daytime. All the little birds except Hooty the Owl and Boomer the Night Hawk, and noisy Mr. Whip-poor-will were fast asleep in their little nests. Old Mother West Wind's Merry Little Breezes had all gone to sleep, too. It was oh so still! Indeed it was so very still that Bobby Coon, coming down the Lone Little Path through the wood, began to talk to himself.

"I don't see what people want to play

all day and sleep all night for," said
Bobby Coon. "Night's the best time
to be about. Now Reddy Fox — "

"Be careful what you say about
Reddy Fox," said a voice right behind
Bobby Coon.

Bobby Coon turned around very
quickly indeed, for he had thought he was
all alone. There was Reddy Fox himself,
trotting down the Lone Little Path
through the wood.

"I thought you were home and fast
asleep, Reddy Fox," said Bobby Coon.

"You were mistaken," said Reddy
Fox, "for you see I'm out to take a walk
in the moonlight."

So Bobby Coon and Reddy Fox walked
together down the Lone Little Path
through the wood to the Green Meadows.
They met Jimmy Skunk, who had
dreamed that there were a lot of beetles
up on the hill, and was just going

to climb the Crooked Little Path to see.

"Hello, Jimmy Skunk!" said Bobby Coon and Reddy Fox. "Come down to the Green Meadows with us."

Jimmy Skunk said he would, so they all went down on the Green Meadows together, Bobby Coon first. Reddy Fox next and Jimmy Skunk last of all, for Jimmy Skunk never hurries. Pretty soon they came to the house of Johnny Chuck.

"Listen," said Bobby Coon, "Johnny Chuck is fast asleep."

They all listened and they could hear Johnny Chuck snoring away down in his snug little bed.

"Let's give Johnny Chuck a surprise," said Reddy Fox.

"What shall it be?" asked Bobby Coon.

"I know," said Reddy Fox. "Let's

roll that big stone right over Johnny Chuck's doorway; then he'll have to dig his way out in the morning."

So Bobby Coon and Reddy Fox pulled and tugged and tugged and pulled at the big stone till they had rolled it over Johnny Chuck's doorway. Jimmy Skunk pretended not to see what they were doing.

"Now let's go down to the Laughing Brook and wake up old Grandfather Frog and hear him say 'Chug-a-rum,'" said Bobby Coon.

"Come on!" cried Reddy Fox, "I'll get there first!"

Away raced Reddy Fox down the Lone Little Path and after him ran Bobby Coon, going to wake old Grandfather Frog from a nice comfortable sleep on his green lily pad.

But Jimmy Skunk didn't go. He watched Reddy Fox and Bobby Coon

until they were nearly to the Laughing
Brook. Then he began to dig at one side
of the big stone which filled the doorway
of Johnny Chuck's house. My, how he
made the dirt fly! Pretty soon he had
made a hole big enough to call through to
Johnny Chuck, who was snoring away,
fast asleep in his snug little bed below.

"Johnny Chuck, Chuck, Chuck!
Johnny Woodchuck!" called Jimmy
Skunk.

But Johnny Chuck just snored.

"Johnny Chuck, Chuck, Chuck!
Johnny Woodchuck!" called Jimmy
Skunk once more.

But Johnny Chuck just snored. Then
Jimmy Skunk called again, this time
louder than before.

"Who is it?" asked a very sleepy
voice.

"It's Jimmy Skunk. Put your coat

on and come up here!" called Jimmy
Skunk.

"Go away, Jimmy Skunk. I want to
sleep!" said Johnny Chuck.

"I've got a surprise for you, Johnny
Chuck. You'd better come!" called
Jimmy Skunk through the little hole he
had made. When Johnny Chuck heard
that Jimmy Skunk had a surprise for
him he wanted to know right away what
it could be, so though he was very, very
sleepy, he put on his coat and started
up for his door to see what the surprise
was that Jimmy Skunk had. And there
he found the big stone Reddy Fox and
Bobby Coon had put there, and of course
he was very much surprised indeed.
He thought Jimmy Skunk had played
him a mean trick and for a few minutes
he was very mad. But Jimmy Skunk
soon told him who had filled up his doorway with the big stone.

"Now you push from that side, Johnny Chuck, and I'll pull from this side, and we'll soon have this big stone out of your doorway," said Jimmy Skunk.

So Johnny Chuck pushed and Jimmy Skunk pulled, and sure enough they soon had the big stone out of Johnny Chuck's doorway.

"Now," said Jimmy Skunk, "we'll roll this big stone down the Lone Little Path to Reddy Fox's house and we'll give Reddy Fox a surprise."

So Johnny Chuck and Jimmy Skunk tugged and pulled and rolled the big stone down to the house of Reddy Fox, and sure enough, it filled his doorway.

"Good night, Jimmy Skunk," said Johnny Chuck, and trotted down the Lone Little Path toward home, chuckling to himself all the way.

Jimmy Skunk walked slowly up the Lone Little Path to the wood, for Jimmy

Skunk never hurries. Pretty soon he came to the big hollow tree where Bobby Coon lives, and there he met Hooty the Owl.

"Hello, Jimmy Skunk, where have you been?" asked Hooty the Owl.

"Just for a walk," said Jimmy Skunk. "Who lives in this big hollow tree?"

Now of course Jimmy Skunk knew all the time, but he pretended he didn't.

"Oh, this is Bobby Coon's house," said Hooty the Owl.

"Let's give Bobby Coon a surprise," said Jimmy Skunk.

"How?" asked Hooty the Owl.

"We'll fill his house full of sticks and leaves," said Jimmy Skunk.

Hooty the Owl thought that would be a good joke, so while Jimmy Skunk gathered all the old sticks and leaves he could find, Hooty the Owl stuffed them into the old hollow tree, which was Bobby

Coon's house, until he couldn't get in another one.

"Good night," said Jimmy Skunk as he began to climb the Crooked Little Path up the hill to his own snug little home.

"Good night," said Hooty the Owl, as he flew like a big soft shadow over to the Great Pine.

By and by when old Mother Moon was just going to bed and all the little stars were too sleepy to twinkle any longer, Reddy Fox and Bobby Coon, very tired and very wet from playing in the Laughing Brook, came up the Lone Little Path, ready to tumble into their snug little beds. They were chuckling over the trick they had played on Johnny Chuck, and the way they had waked up old Grandfather Frog, and all the other mischief they had done. What do you suppose they said when they reached their homes and found that some one else had been playing jokes, too?

I'm sure I don't know, but round, red Mr. Sun was laughing very hard as he peeped over the hill at Reddy Fox and Bobby Coon, and he won't tell why.

XIII

JOHNNY CHUCK FINDS THE BEST THING IN THE WORLD

XIII

JOHNNY CHUCK FINDS THE BEST THING IN THE WORLD

OLD MOTHER WEST WIND had stopped to talk with the Slender Fir Tree.

"I've just come across the Green Meadows," said Old Mother West Wind, "and there I saw the Best Thing in the World."

Striped Chipmunk was sitting under the Slender Fir Tree and he couldn't help hearing what Old Mother West Wind said. "The Best Thing in the World — now what can that be?" thought Striped Chipmunk. "Why, it must be heaps and heaps of nuts and acorns! I'll go and find it."

So Striped Chipmunk started down the Lone Little Path through the wood as fast as he could run. Pretty soon he met Peter Rabbit.

"Where are you going in such a hurry, Striped Chipmunk?" asked Peter Rabbit.

"Down in the Green Meadows to find the Best Thing in the World," replied Striped Chipmunk, and ran faster.

"The Best Thing in the World," said Peter Rabbit, "why, that must be a great pile of carrots and cabbage! I think I'll go and find it."

So Peter Rabbit started down the Lone Little Path through the wood as fast as he could go after Striped Chipmunk.

As they passed the great hollow tree Bobby Coon put his head out. "Where are you going in such a hurry?" asked Bobby Coon.

"Down in the Green Meadows to find the Best Thing in the World!" shouted

"Where are you going in such a hurry, Striped
Chipmunk?" asked Peter Rabbit.

Striped Chipmunk and Peter Rabbit, and both began to run faster.

"The Best Thing in the World," said Bobby Coon to himself, "why, that must be a whole field of sweet milky corn. I think I'll go and find it."

So Bobby Coon climbed down out of the great hollow tree and started down the Lone Little Path through the wood as fast as he could go after Striped Chipmunk and Peter Rabbit, for there is nothing that Bobby Coon likes to eat so well as sweet milky corn.

At the edge of the wood they met Jimmy Skunk.

"Where are you going in such a hurry?" asked Jimmy Skunk.

"Down in the Green Meadows to find the Best Thing in the World!" shouted Striped Chipmunk and Peter Rabbit and Bobby Coon. Then they all tried to run faster.

"The Best Thing in the World," said Jimmy Skunk. "Why, that must be packs and packs of beetles!" And for once in his life Jimmy Skunk began to hurry down the Lone Little Path after Striped Chipmunk and Peter Rabbit and Bobby Coon.

They were all running so fast that they didn't see Reddy Fox until he jumped out of the long grass and asked:

"Where are you going in such a hurry?"

"To find the Best Thing in the World!" shouted Striped Chipmunk and Peter Rabbit and Bobby Coon and Jimmy Skunk, and each did his best to run faster.

"The Best Thing in the World," said Reddy Fox to himself, "Why, that must be a whole pen full of tender young chickens, and I must have them."

So away went Reddy Fox as fast as he could run down the Lone Little Path after Striped Chipmunk, Peter Rabbit, Bobby Coon and Jimmy Skunk.

By and by they all came to the house of Johnny Chuck.

"Where are you going in such a hurry?" asked Johnny Chuck.

"To find the Best Thing in the World," shouted Striped Chipmunk and Peter Rabbit and Bobby Coon and Jimmy Skunk and Reddy Fox.

"The Best Thing in the World," said Johnny Chuck. "Why, I don't know of anything better than my own little home and the warm sunshine and the beautiful blue sky."

So Johnny Chuck stayed at home and played all day among the flowers with the Merry Little Breezes of Old Mother West Wind and was as happy as could be.

But all day long Striped Chipmunk and Peter Rabbit and Bobby Coon and Jimmy Skunk and Reddy Fox ran this way and

ran that way over the Green Meadows
trying to find the Best Thing in the World.
The sun was very, very warm and they
ran so far and they ran so fast that they
were very, very hot and tired, and still
they hadn't found the Best Thing in the
World.

When the long day was over they
started up the Lone Little Path past
Johnny Chuck's house to their own
homes. They didn't hurry now for they
were so very, very tired! And they were
cross — oh so cross! Striped Chipmunk
hadn't found a single nut. Peter Rabbit
hadn't found so much as the leaf of a
cabbage. Bobby Coon hadn't found the
tiniest bit of sweet milky corn. Jimmy
Skunk hadn't seen a single beetle. Reddy
Fox hadn't heard so much as the peep
of a chicken. And all were as hungry as
hungry could be.

Half way up the Lone Little Path they

met Old Mother West Wind going to her home behind the hill. "Did you find the Best Thing in the World?" asked Old Mother West Wind.

"No!" shouted Striped Chipmunk and Peter Rabbit and Bobby Coon and Jimmy Skunk and Reddy Fox all together.

"Johnny Chuck has it," said Old Mother West Wind. "It is being happy with the things you have and not wanting things which some one else has. And it is called Con-tent-ment."

XIV

LITTLE JOE OTTER'S SLIPPERY SLIDE

LITTLE JOE OTTER'S SLIPPERY SLIDE

LITTLE Joe Otter and Billy Mink had been playing together around the Smiling Pool all one sunshiny morning. They had been fishing and had taken home a fine dinner of Trout for old Grandfather Mink and blind old Granny Otter. They had played tag with the Merry Little Breezes. They had been in all kinds of mischief and now they just didn't know what to do.

They were sitting side by side on the Big Rock trying to push each other off into the Smiling Pool. Round, smiling, red Mr. Sun made the Green Meadows very warm indeed, and Reddy Fox, over in the tall grass, heard them splashing and shouting and having such a good time that he wished he liked the nice cool water and could swim, too.

"I've thought of something!" cried Little Joe Otter.

"What is it?" asked Billy Mink.

Little Joe Otter just looked wise and said nothing.

"Something to eat?" asked Billy Mink.

"No," said Little Joe Otter.

"I don't believe you've thought of anything at all," said Billy Mink.

"I have too!" said Little Joe Otter. "It's something to do."

"What?" demanded Billy Mink.

Just then Little Joe Otter spied Jerry Muskrat. "Hi, Jerry Muskrat! Come over here!" he called.

Jerry Muskrat swam across to the Big Rock and climbed up beside Billy Mink and Little Joe Otter.

"What are you fellows doing?" asked Jerry Muskrat.

"Having some fun," said Billy Mink. "Little Joe Otter has thought of something to do, but I don't know what it is."

"Let's make a slide," cried Little Joe Otter.

"You show us how," said Billy Mink.

So Little Joe Otter found a nice smooth place on the bank, and Billy Mink and Jerry Muskrat brought mud and helped him pat it down smooth until they had the loveliest slippery slide in the world. Then Little Joe Otter climbed up the bank to the top of the slippery slide and lay down flat on his stomach. Billy Mink gave him a push and away he went down, down the slippery slide, splash into the Smiling Pool. Then Jerry Muskrat tried it and after him Billy Mink. Then all did it over again. Sometimes they went down the slippery slide on their backs, sometimes flat on their stomachs, sometimes head first, sometimes feet first. Oh such fun as they did have! Even Grandfather Frog came over and tried the slippery slide.

Johnny Chuck, over in the Green Meadows, heard the noise and stole down the Lone Little Path to see. Jimmy Skunk, looking for beetles up on the hill, heard the noise and forgot that he hadn't had his breakfast. Reddy Fox, taking a nap, woke up and hurried over to watch the fun. Last of all came Peter Rabbit.

Little Joe Otter saw him coming. "Hello, Peter Rabbit!" he shouted. "Come and try the slippery slide."

Now Peter Rabbit couldn't swim, but he pretended that he didn't want to.

"I've left my bathing suit at home," said Peter Rabbit.

"Never mind," said Billy Mink. "Mr. Sun will dry you off."

"And we'll help," said all the Merry Little Breezes of Old Mother West Wind.

But Peter Rabbit shook his head and said, "No."

Faster and faster went Billy Mink and Little Joe Otter and Jerry Muskrat and old Grandfather Frog down the slippery slide into the Smiling Pool.

Peter Rabbit kept coming near and nearer until finally he stood right at the top of the slippery slide. Billy Mink crept up behind him very softly and gave him a push. Peter Rabbit's long legs flew out from under him and down he sat with a thump on the slippery slide. "Oh," cried Peter Rabbit, and tried to stop himself. But he couldn't do it and so away he went down the slippery slide, splash into the Smiling Pool.

"Ha! ha! ha!" laughed Billy Mink.

"Ho! ho! ho!" shouted Little Joe Otter.

"He! he! he!" laughed Jerry Muskrat and old Grandfather Frog and Sammy Jay and Jimmy Skunk and Reddy Fox and Blacky the Crow and Mr. Kingfisher, for you know Peter Rabbit was forever playing jokes on them.

Poor Peter Rabbit! The water got in his eyes and up his nose and into his mouth and made him choke and splutter, and then he couldn't get back on the bank, for you know Peter Rabbit couldn't swim.

When Little Joe Otter saw what a dreadful time Peter Rabbit was having he dove into the Smiling Pool and took hold of one of Peter Rabbit's long ears. Billy Mink swam out and took hold of the other long ear. Jerry Muskrat swam right under Peter Rabbit and took him on his back. Then with old Grandfather Frog swimming ahead they took Peter Rabbit right across the Smiling Pool and pulled him out on the grassy bank, where it was nice and warm. All the Merry Little Breezes of Old Mother West Wind came over and helped Mr Sun dry Peter Rabbit off.

Then they all sat down together and watched Little Joe Otter turn a somersault down the slippery slide.

XV

THE TALE OF TOMMY TROUT WHO DIDN'T MIND

THE TALE OF TOMMY TROUT WHO DIDN'T MIND

IN the Laughing Brook, which ripples and sings all day long, lived Mr. Trout and Mrs. Trout, and a whole lot of little Trouts. There were so many little Trouts that Mr. Trout and Mrs. Trout were kept very busy indeed getting breakfast and dinner and supper for them, and watching out for them and teaching them how to swim and how to catch foolish little flies that sometimes fell on the water and how to keep out of the way of big hungry fish and sharp eyed Mr. Kingfisher and big men and little boys who came fishing with hooks and lines.

Now all the little Trouts were very, very good and minded just what Mrs. Trout told them — all but Tommy Trout, for Tommy Trout — oh, dear, dear! Tommy Trout never could mind right away. He always had to wait a little instead of minding when he was spoken to.

Tommy Trout didn't mean to be bad. Oh dear, no! He just wanted to have his own way, and because Tommy Trout had his own way and didn't mind Mrs. Trout there isn't any Tommy Trout now. No sir, there isn't as much as one little blue spot of his beautiful little coat left because —why, just because Tommy Trout didn't mind.

One day when round, red Mr. Sun was shining and the Laughing Brook was singing on its way to join the Big River, Mrs. Trout started out to get some nice plump flies for dinner. All the little

Mrs. Trout started out to get some nice plump
flies for dinner.

Trouts were playing in their dear little pool, safe behind the Big Rock. Before she started Mrs. Trout called all the little Trouts around her and told them not to leave their little pool while she was gone, "For," said she, "something dreadful might happen to you."

All the little Trouts, except Tommy Trout, promised that they would surely, surely stay inside their dear little pool. Then they all began to jump and chase each other and play as happy as could be, all but Tommy Trout.

As soon as Mrs. Trout had started Tommy Trout swam off by himself to the edge of the pool. "I wonder what is on the other side of the Big Rock," said Tommy Trout. "The sun is shining and the brook is laughing and nothing could happen if I go just a little speck of a ways."

So, when no one was looking, Tommy

Trout slipped out of the safe little pool where all the other little Trouts were playing. He swam just a little speck of a ways. But he couldn't see around the Big Rock. So he swam just a little speck of a ways farther still. Now he could see almost around the Big Rock. Then he swam just a little speck of a ways farther and—oh dear, dear! he looked right into the mouth of a great big, big fish called Mr. Pickerel, who is very fond of little Trouts and would like to eat one for breakfast every day.

"Ah ha!" said Mr. Pickerel, opening his big, big mouth very, very wide.

Tommy Trout turned to run back to the dear, dear safe little pool where all the other little Trouts were playing so happily, but he was too late. Into that great big, big mouth he went instead, and Mr. Pickerel swallowed him whole.

"Ah ha," said Mr. Pickerel, "I like little Trouts."

And nothing more was ever heard of Tommy Trout, who didn't mind.

XVI

SPOTTY THE TURTLE WINS A RACE

SPOTTY THE TURTLE WINS A RACE

ALL the little people who live on the Green Meadows and in the Smiling Pool and along the Laughing Brook were to have a holiday. The Merry Little Breezes of Old Mother West Wind had been very busy, oh, very busy indeed, in sending word to all the little meadow folks. You see, Peter Rabbit had been boasting of how fast he could run. Reddy Fox was quite sure that he could run faster than Peter Rabbit. Billy Mink, who can move so quickly you hardly can see him, was quite sure that neither Peter Rabbit nor Reddy Fox could run as fast as he. They all met one day beside the Smiling Pool and agreed that old Grandfather Frog should decide who was the swiftest.

Now Grandfather Frog was accounted very wise. You see he had lived a long time, oh, very much longer than any of the others, and therefore, because of the wisdom of age, Grandfather Frog was always called on to decide all disputes. He sat on his green lily-pad while Billy Mink sat on the Big Rock, and Peter Rabbit and Reddy Fox sat on the bank. Each in turn told why he thought he was the fastest. Old Grandfather Frog listened and listened and said never a word until they were all through. When they had finished, he stopped to catch a foolish green fly and then he said:

"The best way to decide who is the swiftest is to have a race."

So it was agreed that Peter Rabbit and Reddy Fox and Billy Mink should start together from the old butternut tree on one edge of the Green Meadows, race away across the Green Meadows to the little hill on the other side and each bring back a nut from the big hickory which grew there. The one who first reached the old butternut tree with a hickory nut would be declared the winner. The Merry Little Breezes flew about over the Green Meadows telling every one about the race and every one planned to be there.

It was a beautiful summer day. Mr. Sun smiled and smiled, and the more he smiled the warmer it grew. Every one was there to see the race—Striped Chipmunk, Happy Jack Squirrel, Sammy Jay, Blacky the Crow, Hooty the Owl and Bobby Coon all sat up in the old butternut tree where it was cool and shady. Johnny Chuck, Jerry Muskrat, Jimmy Skunk, Little Joe Otter, Grandfather Frog and even old Mr. Toad, were there. Last of all came Spotty the Turtle. Now Spotty the Turtle is a very slow walker and he cannot run at all. When Peter Rabbit saw him coming up towards the old butternut tree he shouted: "Come, Spotty, don't you want to race with us?"

Everybody laughed because you know Spotty is so very, very slow; but Spotty didn't laugh and he didn't get cross because every one else laughed.

"There is a wise old saying, Peter Rabbit," said Spotty the Turtle, "which shows that those who run fastest do not always reach a place first. I think I *will* enter this race."

Every one thought that that was the best joke they had heard for a long time, and all laughed harder than ever. They all agreed that Spotty the Turtle should start in the race too.

So they all stood in a row, Peter Rabbit first, then Billy Mink, then Reddy Fox, and right side of Reddy Fox Spotty the Turtle.

"Are you ready?" asked Grandfather Frog. "Go!"

Away went Peter Rabbit with great big jumps. After him went Billy Mink so fast that he was just a little brown streak going through the tall grass, and side by side with him ran Reddy Fox. Now just as they started Spotty the Turtle reached up and grabbed the long hair on the end of Reddy's big tail. Of course Reddy couldn't have stopped to shake him off, because Peter Rabbit and Billy Mink were running so fast that he had to run his very best to keep up with them. But he didn't even know that Spotty the Turtle was there. You see Spotty is not very heavy and Reddy Fox was so excited that he did not notice that his big tail was heavier than usual.

The Merry Little Breezes flew along,

too, to see that the race was fair. Peter Rabbit went with great big jumps. Whenever he came to a little bush he jumped right over it, for Peter Rabbit's legs are long and meant for jumping. Billy Mink is so slim that he slipped between the bushes and through the long grass like a little brown streak. Reddy Fox, who is bigger than either Peter Rabbit or Billy Mink, had no trouble in keeping up with them. Not one of them noticed that Spotty the Turtle was hanging fast to the end of Reddy's tail.

Now just at the foot of the little hill on which the big hickory tree grew was a little pond. It wasn't very wide but it was quite long. Billy Mink remembered this pond and he chuckled to himself as he raced along, for he knew that Peter Rabbit couldn't swim and he knew that Reddy Fox does not like the water, so therefore both would have to run around it. He himself can swim even faster than he can run. The more he thought of this, the more foolish it seemed that he should hurry so on such a warm day. "For," said Billy Mink to himself, "even if they reach the pond first, they will have to run around it, while I can swim across it and cool off while I am swimming. I will surely get there first." So Billy Mink ran slower and slower, and pretty soon he had dropped behind.

Mr. Sun, round and red, looking down, smiled and smiled to see the race. The more he smiled the warmer it grew. Now Peter Rabbit had a thick gray coat and Reddy Fox had a thick red coat, and they both began to get very, very warm. Peter Rabbit did not make such long jumps as when he first started. Reddy Fox began to feel very thirsty, and his tongue hung out. Now that Billy

Mink was behind them they thought they did not need to hurry so.

Peter Rabbit reached the little pond first. He had not thought of that pond when he agreed to enter the race. He stopped right on the edge of it and sat up on his hind legs. Right across he could see the big hickory tree, so near and yet so far, for he knew that he must run around the pond and then back again, and it was a long, long way. In just a moment Reddy Fox ran out of the bushes and Reddy felt very much as Peter Rabbit did. Way, way behind them was Billy Mink, trotting along comfortably and chuckling to himself. Peter Rabbit looked at Reddy Fox in dismay, and Reddy Fox looked at Peter Rabbit in dismay. Then they both looked at Billy Mink and remembered that Billy Mink could swim right across.

Then off Peter Rabbit started as fast

as he could go around the pond one way,
and Reddy Fox started around the pond
the other way. They were so excited
that neither noticed a little splash in the
pond. That was Spotty the Turtle
who had let go of Reddy's tail and now
was swimming across the pond, for you
know that Spotty is a splendid swimmer.
Only once or twice he stuck his little
black nose up to get some air. The rest
of the time he swam under water and no
one but the Merry Little Breezes saw him.
Right across he swam, and climbed up
the bank right under the big hickory
tree.

Now there were just three nuts left
under the hickory tree. Two of these
Spotty took down to the edge of the pond
and buried in the mud. The other he
took in his mouth and started back across
the pond. Just as he reached the other
shore up trotted Billy Mink, but Billy

Mink didn't see Spotty. He was too intent watching Reddy Fox and Peter Rabbit, who were now half way around the pond. In he jumped with a splash. My! How good that cool water did feel! He didn't have to hurry now, because he felt sure that the race was his. So he swam round and round and chased some fish and had a beautiful time in the water. By and by he looked up and saw that Peter Rabbit was almost around the pond one way and Reddy Fox was almost around the pond the other way. They both looked tired and hot and discouraged.

Then Billy Mink swam slowly across and climbed out on the bank under the big hickory tree. But where were the nuts? Look as he would, he could not see a nut anywhere, yet the Merry Little Breezes had said there were three nuts lying under the hickory tree. Billy Mink ran this way and ran that way. He was still running around, poking over the leaves and looking under the twigs and pieces of bark when Peter Rabbit and Reddy Fox came up.

Then they, too, began to look under the leaves and under the bark. They pawed around in the grass, they hunted in every nook and cranny, but not a nut could they find. They were tired and cross and hot and they accused Billy Mink of having hidden the nuts. Billy Mink stoutly insisted that he had not hidden the nuts, that he had not found the nuts, and when they saw how hard he was hunting they believed him.

All the afternoon they hunted and hunted and hunted, and all the afternoon Spotty the Turtle, with the nut in his mouth, was slowly, oh, so slowly, crawling straight back across the Green Meadows towards the old butternut tree.

Round, red Mr. Sun was getting very close to the Purple Hills, where he goes to bed every night, and all the little meadow folks were getting ready to go to their homes. They were wondering and wondering what could have happened to the racers, when Sammy Jay spied the Merry Little Breezes dancing across the Green Meadows.

"Here come the Merry Little Breezes; they'll tell us who wins the race," cried Sammy Jay.

When the Merry Little Breezes reached the old butternut tree, all the little meadow folks crowded around them, but the Merry Little Breezes just laughed and laughed and wouldn't say a word. Then all of a sudden, out of the tall meadow grass crept Spotty the Turtle and laid the hickory nut at the feet of old Grandfather Frog. Old Grandfather Frog was so surprised that he actually let a great green fly buzz right past his nose.

"Where did you get that hickory nut?" asked Grandfather Frog.

"Under the big hickory tree on the hill on the other side of the Green Meadows," said Spotty.

Then all the Merry Little Breezes clapped their hands and shouted: "He did! He did! Spotty wins the race!"

Then they told how Spotty reached the pond by clinging to the tip of Reddy Fox's tail, and had hidden the other two nuts, and then how he had patiently crawled home while Billy Mink and Reddy Fox and Peter Rabbit were hunting and hunting and hunting for the nuts they could not find.

And so Spotty the Turtle was awarded the race, and to this day Peter Rabbit and Reddy Fox and Billy Mink can't bear the sight of a hickory nut.